SCOOBY-DOO!

MUMMIES AT THE MALL

By Gail Herman

Illustrated by Duendes del Sur

SCHOLASTIC INC.

New York   Toronto   London   Auckland   Sydney
Mexico City   New Delhi   Hong Kong   Buenos Aires

ISBN 0-439-34114-0

12 11 10   3 4 5 6/0

Designed by Maria Stasavage
Printed in the U.S.A.
First Scholastic printing, May 2002

The Coolsville Mall was packed.
Scooby-Doo, Shaggy, and the gang
stood in a crowd of people.
"Let's figure out what we want to
do," said Shaggy, "before we get
squeezed any tighter."

All at once, the crowd moved through a set of doors.

"Oh!" said Daphne. "We're in front of the movie theater."

"The movie must be about to start," said Velma.

Fred nodded. "We should go!"

Shaggy pointed to the movie poster. "*Mummies on the Loose* is playing." He shivered. "Like, we'll catch you later. Scoob and I will find something else to do."

Shaggy and Scooby stopped in a
pet store.
Two dogs were being groomed.
"Care for a day of beauty?" Shaggy
asked Scooby.
Scooby shook his head. "Ro way!"

Next they went to a store called Snooze City. Shaggy and Scooby gazed at the cozy beds, soft pillows, and thick blankets. Scooby yawned. Shaggy stretched. "Forty winks sounds pretty good to me. What do you think, good buddy?"

"Good buddy?" Shaggy whirled around. Scooby wasn't there! Then Shaggy spotted him. He had run outside. He was seated in front of a giant hot dog.

"Hey, that's just a guy in costume," said Shaggy. The hot dog guy handed Shaggy a flyer.

"'All-You-Can-Eat Day at Coolsville Mall,'" Shaggy read. "'Go to any restaurant! EAT till you're stuffed! All for one price!'"

"First stop, Big Burger!"
Shaggy shouted,
leading Scooby into
a restaurant. The hours
passed, burger by burger.

Finally, Scooby and Shaggy came out.
Scooby patted his belly.
"Had enough?" Shaggy
asked. "Well, just
in case, I stashed
some burgers
in my pockets."

BIG BURGER

Next came Hot Dog Hut, then Sausage Shack. Each time it was the same. The friends stuffed themselves. Then Shaggy stuffed his pockets!

Finally, they waddled out of the Barbecue Pit. "That mummy movie will be over soon," Shaggy said to Scooby. "Let's go meet the gang."

All at once, shouts rang through the mall. Heavy footsteps echoed all around. *Thud, thud.*

THUD! They grew louder and louder. Scooby's ears quivered.

"Hey, relax, good buddy." Shaggy laughed.
"Look — it's just the hot dog guy!"
But something was behind him. *Two*
somethings! Wrapped in bandages!
"Rummies!" yelled Scooby.
"Mummies!" yelled Shaggy.

"The mummies are chasing the hot dog guy," Shaggy said. "So we should be safe." But the hot dog guy had disappeared. Now the mummies were after *them*.

"Zoinks!" yelled Shaggy. "Run!"

The chase was on . . . past the restaurants . . . past Snooze City. There were pillows everywhere. "The mummies must have torn this place up!" said Shaggy.

They raced past the pet store.
The mummies had struck
there, too!

Shaggy pointed to a sports store. "Let's hide in there!" The buddies ran inside. They twisted around to check for the mummies. *CRASH!* They slammed into a huge pile of tennis balls.

Balls rolled everywhere. Shaggy and Scooby couldn't run. They couldn't even stand.

The mummies were coming closer! Finally, Shaggy and Scooby grabbed tennis rackets.

"Service!" shouted Shaggy as they swung at balls and cleared a path. "Now let's go!"

"Quick!" Shaggy called to Scooby. "In here!" They raced into Coolsville Clothes. They slipped into big coats and floppy hats. "Great disguise!" said Shaggy. "The mummies will never find us now!"

Thud, thud! "Rikes!" Scooby cried. The mummies were smarter than they thought. They were coming toward them!

Shaggy and Scooby sped out the door.

"There's the gang!" said Shaggy.

Scooby jumped into Daphne's arms.

"Excuse me, sir," said Daphne.

"Can I help you?"

MOVIES

TICKETS

"You can help *us*!" said Shaggy. He and
Scooby whipped off their disguises.
      "What's going on?" asked Fred.

In a flash, Shaggy explained about the mummies. How they made a mess at the pet store and Snooze City. How they chased the hot dog guy, and now were chasing them.

"Hmmmm," said Velma, thinking it over.

Then Fred wrinkled his nose. "What's that smell?"

Shaggy pulled out hamburgers and hot dogs from his pockets. "Leftovers!"
Just then a pet store worker ran over.
"Have you seen King and Queen?" he asked.
"Two of our dogs disappeared."

"Oh, no!" wailed Shaggy.
"The mummies got them!"
Thud, thud!
"And here they come —
for us!"

Velma stepped in between Shaggy, Scooby, and the mummies. She held up her hand. "Stay!"
The mummies stopped.
"Wow," said Shaggy. "Those mummies are good listeners!"

"They're not mummies," Velma said.
"They're King and Queen, and I think
they're hungry. They must have
thought the hot dog guy was a real
hot dog, and the
two of you smell
like . . . well . . ."
She pointed to the
food. "Like lunch."

"But they sure look like mummies," Shaggy said.

Velma pulled off the bandages. "These are sheets. They must have run into Snooze City and gotten wrapped up while they were making a mess."

"Poor things," said Daphne.

Shaggy looked at Scooby and shrugged. Then he gave the dogs all the food. "There goes our snack." He sighed. "But I'm not afraid of mummies anymore!"

"Hey, Scoob. How about
we get some popcorn?"
"Scooby-Dooby-Doo!"